HANDS OFF!

Mario Mariotti

A CRANKY NELL BOOK

Kane/Miller Book Publishers

Brooklyn, New York & La Jolla, California

Idea and artistic realizations by Mario Mariotti
in collaboration with Francesca Mariotti.

Original photographs by Roberto Marchiori.

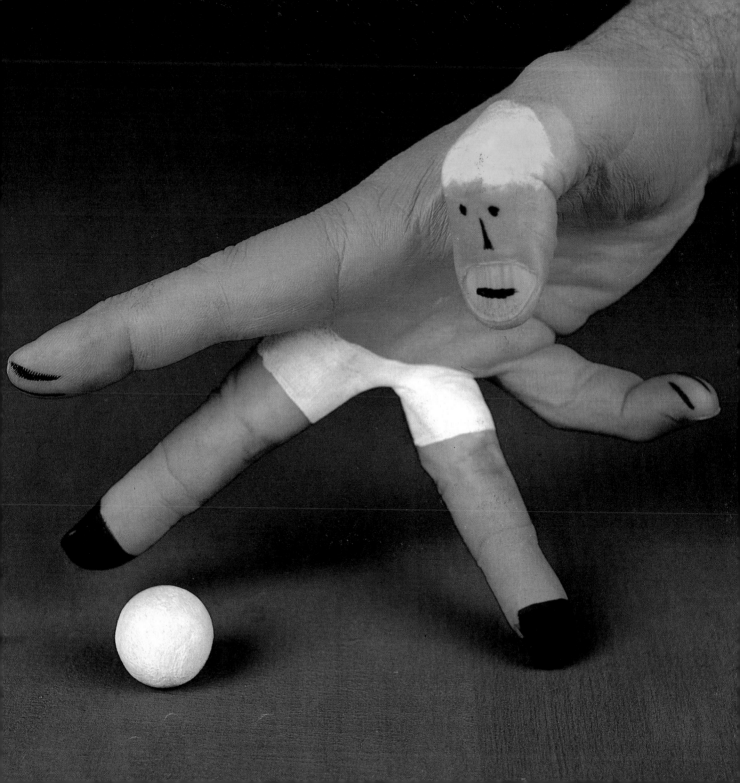

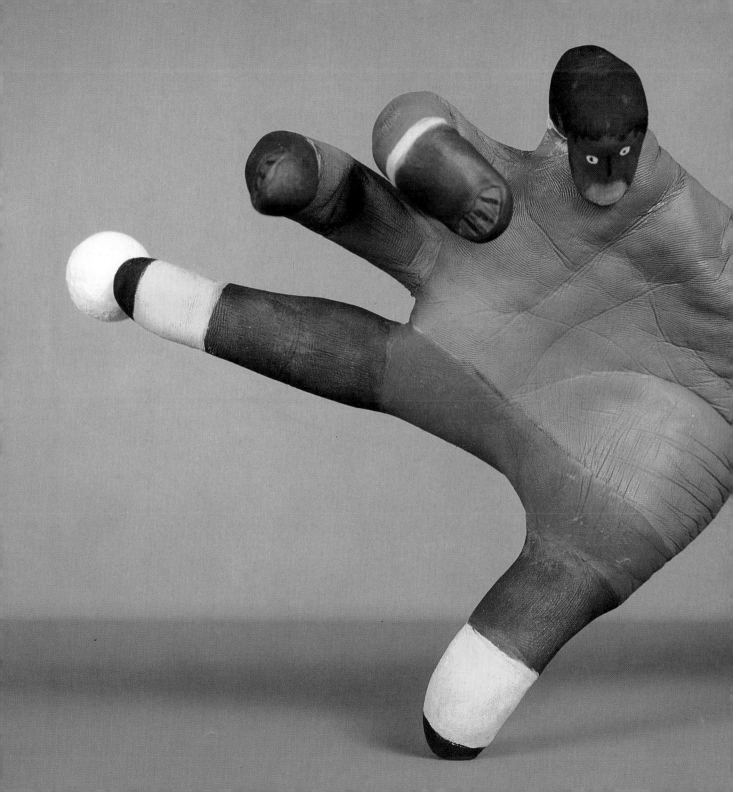

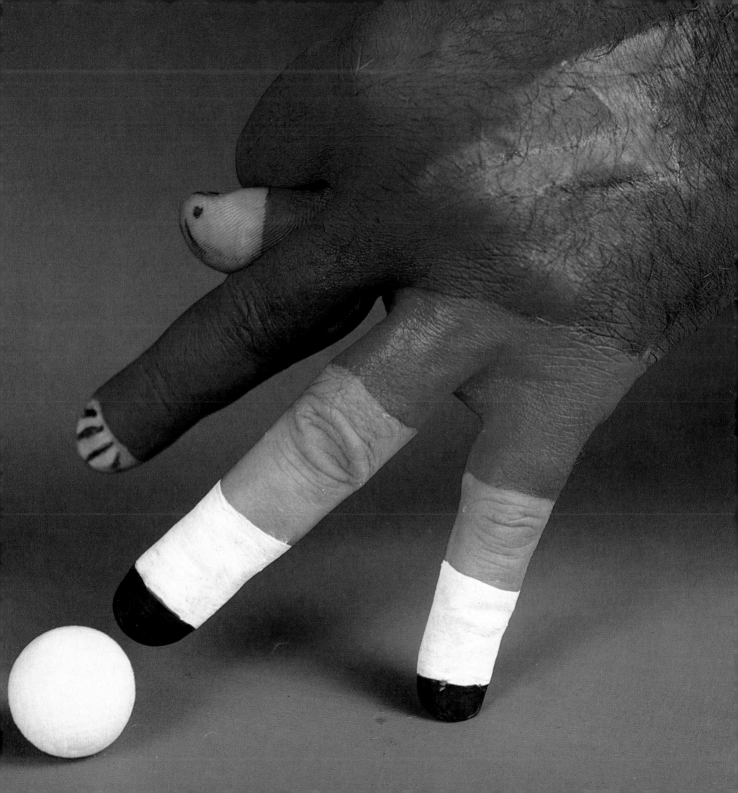

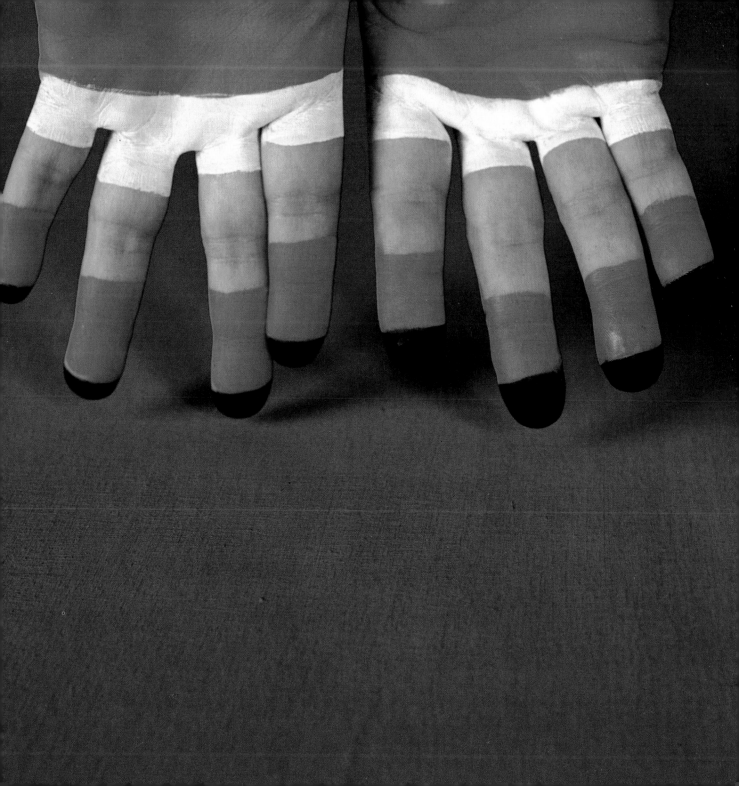

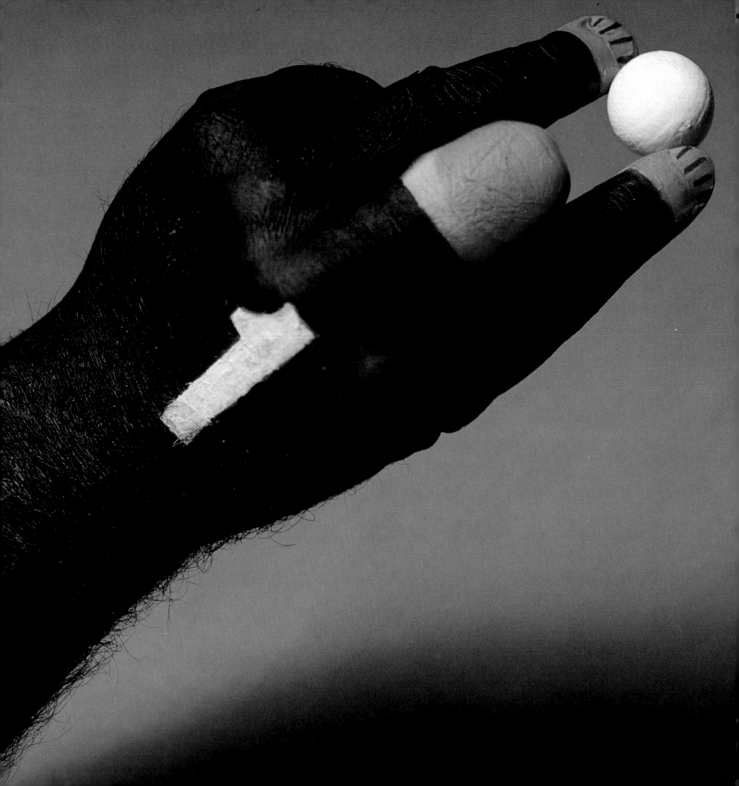

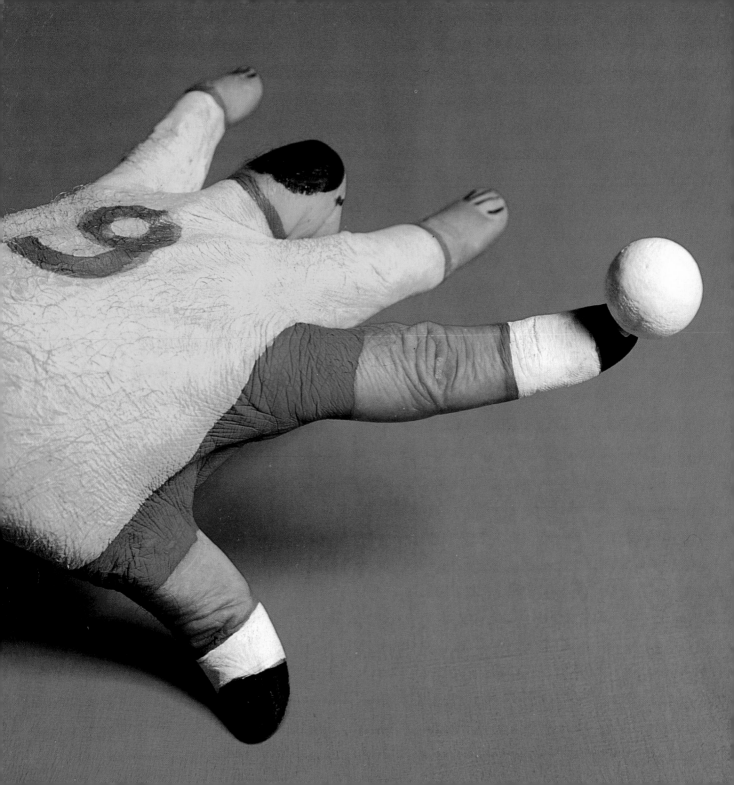

Hands Off! is a central idea of the game of soccer, where one can use any and all parts of one's body save for the hands (the goalie, of course, being the notable exception). However, the use of one's hands happens to be central to my books HANIMALS, HUMANDS, HANIMATIONS) and to my livelihood, and thus, at the risk of being called for a foul, I have used my hands to create the soccer game that unfolds throughout the pages of this book. In fact, HANDS OFF! could quite possibly be my most *hands on* book in the complexity and intricacy of characters and action.

I advise you too to risk a foul by using your hands to run through the pages of this book and become part of the game in progress. You can mirror my hands or create new players and some plays of your own. HANDS OFF! yes, but only after you make your hands into feet.

MARIO MARIOTTI